GOLD MOUNTAIN

A STORY ABOUT GOLD RUSH DAYS IN OREGON

By Gwendolyn Lampshire Hayden
and Pearl Clements Gischler

Cover design by Elle Staples

Cover illustration by Colista Dowling and Tatiana Glebova

Inside Illustrations by Colista Dowling

This unabridged version has updated grammar and spelling.

Originally titled *Muslin Town*

First published in 1946

© 2018 Jenny Phillips

goodandbeautiful.com

Dedicated To Our Parents

Real Pioneers

Table of Contents

1. Creaking Wheels 1

2. Gold! 13

3. Red-Flannel Mine 20

4. Muslin Town. 31

5. Winter 45

6. Garden On Gold Mountain. 57

7. A New Betsy Ross. 69

CHAPTER 1

Creaking Wheels

"Goodbye! Goodbye!" called Daniel and Betsy. They waved again and again to all the folks standing by the garden gate.

"Goodbye, Grandpa and Grandma Lane. Goodbye, Uncle Will and Aunt Sue. Goodbye, cousins!"

The two children watched and waved until the figures grew smaller and smaller. At last the big, white-topped wagon rolled slowly around a bend in the dusty road. Then they could no longer see their old farm.

Daniel and Betsy blinked their blue eyes before they looked at each other. Pa had said that they must not cry when they left their nice farm. They must be happy all the way down the wide valley and across the Cascade Mountains. They must smile as they went up, up into the Blue Mountains of eastern Oregon.

"Your Ma will soon get well and strong in the beautiful Blue Mountains," Pa told them. "Up there the air is clear and cool. We will have very little rainfall. Even cold winter days are sunny. Sun and snow will bring back the roses to Ma's cheeks. And perhaps we can earn enough money over there to buy another farm."

"We are real pioneers now," boasted Daniel. "This is just the way Pa and Ma came all the long miles out to the WEST from the East."

"Yes," giggled Betsy. "Only we are 'backward' pioneers because we are coming from the West and going toward the EAST."

They began to laugh. They laughed and laughed until Calico Cat woke up from her nap in Betsy's lap. She blinked her green eyes. She yawned with wide-open mouth and stretched her gray back.

Sleepy Rags growled a low dog-growl deep in his throat. He lifted his head from his paws. He rolled his big brown eyes and looked up into Daniel's face.

Ma heard all the noise. She turned around from the high wagon seat and smiled at them. Her pale cheeks were now pink from excitement.

"Don't be too noisy, children," her soft voice called. "You might frighten our animals. You see, they do not know about our plans. They must wonder why we are going down this strange road."

Daniel and Betsy looked back at Mercy-Me, the brindle cow. Pa had given her this queer name. He did so because Ma jumped back very quickly whenever the cow shook her long, sharp horns. Then Ma always said, "Oh, mercy me!"

They looked at Hope, Pa's saddle mare. Pa was such a funny man. He had chosen this queer name, too. He said it was because he could only HOPE that his horse did not buck him off. But she was really very tame. She did not buck at all.

Mercy-Me and Hope were tied to the back of the wagon. They walked slowly along in the warm June sunshine. Pa and Ma, Daniel and Betsy, Calico and Rags, and the cooped-up chickens rode under the white canvas top. The two big oxen, Tick and Tack, pulled the heavy load.

They always stopped at noon for a cold lunch while the animals rested and ate grass. Each night Pa found a good camping place. He built a fire and then milked the cow while Ma cooked a hot supper. The children drank all of the warm, foaming milk that they could hold. They gave the rest of it to Calico and Rags and the beautiful Barred Rock rooster and the six hens.

Each morning Ma cooked a good breakfast while Pa milked Mercy-Me. The morning milk was poured into a small wooden keg. All day long the keg rocked back and forth on the side of the jolting wagon. The rocking churned the rich cream into butter. Every night they had a golden ball of butter to spread on the thick slices of homemade bread that Ma had baked before leaving home.

Day after day they rode along. They went through towns Pa and Ma had seen nine years ago when they had first come up the broad Willamette Valley on their way to settle far up the river at Eugene City. Corvallis, Albany, Salem, and Oregon City. All of these, except Oregon City, were on the flat valley floor. Pa and Ma talked about how much these towns had grown since they had first seen them.

"Someday there will be farms all over this fertile valley," Pa said.

"Yes, and towns, too, and even cities," Ma added. "And there will be fine roads and good bridges. Perhaps there will even be railroads!"

Near Portland they camped for two days and

rested the oxen. It would be a long, hard journey up the Columbia River and over the high Cascade Mountains. The sagebrush desert which lay beyond was hot and dry. Plenty of supplies had to be bought, for on the other side of the Cascades, there would be fewer and fewer places where they could buy food and clothing.

One late afternoon, as the old oxen wound wearily down a dim wagon trail through the desert, Daniel and Betsy saw three far-away specks following them in a cloud of dust.

The specks quickly grew larger and larger.

"Pa!" called Betsy. "Here come three men. Their horses are galloping as fast as they can."

"Yes, and they are the very same men who stopped at our camp yesterday and asked us where we were going!" Daniel added excitedly as the riders drew closer.

Ma's soft voice did not grow any louder as she kept on talking to Pa and turned halfway around on the high wagon seat to glance back. But Betsy saw a frightened look in her eyes.

Pa pulled Tick and Tack to a stop as the nearest man dashed up and jerked his horse to a sudden halt.

"Well, hello there, Lane!" said the black-bearded rider. "We didn't know this was your outfit. It's sure a surprise to come across you folks again. How about making camp with you tonight?"

His sharp eyes stared at each of them before he turned to scowl at growling Rags.

Daniel and Betsy saw Pa look closely at the men's lather-covered horses before he answered. Daniel's keen gaze noticed the sparkle of a queer-looking gold watch chain that stretched across the man's broad chest. Betsy looked at the black and white plaid trousers worn by the stranger.

Pa looked out across the lonely desert and then back at the man.

"I guess it'll be all right," he said slowly. But the children noticed that he did not smile as he spoke.

The two parties rode along for an hour before

They stuffed the heavy money bag into Dear Melissa's half-empty body.

finding a good stopping place. As Pa made camp a short distance ahead of the three strangers, he called Daniel and Betsy together.

"I don't like the looks of those men," Pa whispered. "They may be after our money pouch. They might try to rob us in the night. Such things have happened, you know. We don't have much money, and we surely need what we do have. It may be a long time before I can earn any more. So I think that we had better hide the money somewhere. But I can't decide on a safe hiding place. We mustn't mention a word about all of this to Ma, though, for she would worry. We must let her think that everything is all right."

Betsy looked down thoughtfully at Dear Melissa, her button-eyed rag doll.

"Here!" she exclaimed, holding up her treasured toy. "I can open up this little mended place in her body just as easy as anything. Then we can stick the pouch right inside the place where the sawdust leaked out."

Pa laughed aloud as he patted Betsy's cheek and

pulled one of her long red braids.

"You're a smart little girl," he said proudly, as they stuffed the heavy money bag into Dear Melissa's half-empty body and buttoned up her ruffled dress.

"Now, Melissa," said Betsy, fondly patting her doll. "You can go right to bed. You have had your supper. You are full of money."

The sun was well up the next morning before Pa called Ma to tell her that breakfast was ready.

"Why didn't you call me earlier, Joseph?" Ma asked, as she rubbed her sleepy eyes and looked around.

"Oh, I thought you needed to sleep longer, after all the excitement we had in the middle of the night. I have never heard Rags bark as much as he did along about midnight. I guess he was just saying farewell to our unwelcome guests."

"Have they gone?" Ma asked in surprise.

"Yes, I figure they left while Rags was barking

so loudly."

"Look at Rags!" Daniel's shrill voice called out. "What is he doing?"

They all turned to see the dog. He was snarling and biting at something between his paws. Even Calico Cat watched closely, her ears pricked up and her tail twitching back and forth.

"It's a piece of cloth!" Betsy cried.

Daniel ran forward and grabbed the dog's plaything. "Why, he has a piece of that man's checked pants. That's what this is."

"So it is!" Pa said slowly, as he turned the ragged piece of cloth over and over in his hands. "It must be the seat right out of Mr. Black-Beard's trousers."

Then Pa patted Rags on his shaggy head and called him a good dog.

After breakfast, when Betsy and Danny were busy feeding the chickens, Pa came around the wagon. "How's Dear Melissa, Betsy?" Pa asked with a big grin.

"Still full of money, Pa," Betsy replied proudly. "I slept all night with her hugged up tight against me."

"Yes, I know," Pa said. "I was watching. I guess we have Melissa and Rags to thank for saving our money. After this, we will be a little more careful about the kind of company that we allow in our camp. We can't afford to risk another robbery!"

As the creaking wheels again rolled forward on the journey, Betsy kissed Dear Melissa, and Daniel hugged Rags.

"You have both been real heroes," Betsy said to them. "Haven't they, Danny?"

"They certainly have!" agreed Daniel, nodding his head.

Rags thumped his tail against the wagon's endgate as if to say that he quite agreed.

CHAPTER 2

Gold!

After many days of travel through the sage and over mountains, the ox team at last pulled the big covered wagon into a deep, green valley. A rushing stream ran singing along between the high, rocky hills. Along its banks grew beautiful cottonwood and pine trees. Bunchgrass as high as Pa's knees grew in the valleys. Blue and pink and yellow wildflowers peeked out of the tall waving grasses. Dainty flowers bloomed in shady places.

"Oh, look!" cried Betsy. "I see two men down by the creek. They are kneeling by the edge of the water. What are they doing?"

"Each one is shaking a big, flat pan back and forth," added Daniel, leaning far out of the back of the wagon.

"Bow-wow-wow," barked Rags. He jumped out over the endgate. He dashed toward the men, barking in a loud, angry tone. One of the men dropped his heavy, flat pan. He grabbed his gun. Then he looked up and saw their wagon, with Mercy-Me and Hope tied to the back. He spoke to Rags, who stopped barking and wagged his tail. After the man bent over and patted Rags, he raised up and waved his hand to the newcomers. The two men walked over to the wagon.

"Howdy-do," said the man who had patted Rags. "My name is Allred. ALL-RED. That is an easy name to say. But this man has a harder name. He is called Macgruder."

Pa and Ma smiled at the friendly strangers. Then Pa climbed down from the wagon seat and shook hands with them.

"I am Joseph Lane," he said. "And this is my wife, Mary Lou Lane." Ma smiled again and nodded politely.

"This little redhead is Betsy. And the black-haired half-pint is Daniel."

Mr. Allred looked at them. Then he looked up at tall Pa. He winked one eye at the children before he spoke.

"Well, well," he said, turning to Macgruder. "Didn't I tell you today that we needed good roads in here so that a pack train could bring in food for our camp? And here we have them already."

Daniel and Betsy stared at each other. Their eyes opened wide. Their eyebrows lifted up in half circles. What did he mean? They had traveled over an old, rough trail to reach this place. There were no good, smooth roads here.

Mr. Allred chuckled. This time he winked the other eye at them.

"Don't you see what I mean?" he asked, pointing first to tall Pa and then to the small children. "Now we have a long Lane and two short Lanes in our camp."

Then all of them laughed before Mr. Allred went on talking.

"We've struck gold here," he announced.

"Gold!" exclaimed Pa.

"Gold!!" gasped Ma.

"Gold!!!" shouted Daniel and Betsy.

"Yes, that's right. We've struck gold." He took a little bottle out of his pocket and handed it to Pa. Daniel and Betsy saw the little grains of gold roll around as Pa turned the bottle back and forth, up and down.

"Soon many people will come to this place to stake out claims," Mr. Allred went on. "Lane, why don't you stake a claim?"

"We've struck gold!" He took a little bottle out of his pocket.

"Certainly," added Macgruder. "Why don't you! We'll find as much gold right here in this little part of eastern Oregon as the miners have dug up in the whole state of California. Anyway, that is my guess."

Pa looked all around. There were no houses. There were no stores. There was nothing but the trees and the grass and the rushing river and themselves.

Pa shook his head.

"I can't stay long," he said. "This is no place for my wife to live—"

He looked at Ma. Ma's eyes were shining. She held out her hand, and Pa helped her down from the wagon. Then she looked all around just as Pa had done.

"Why not stay here, Joseph?" she asked. "This is as nice a place as we will find. The high hills will keep out the strong wind. The creek will give us pure, cold water to drink. We can put our wagon under those big trees until we can build a good shelter. Just see how tall the flowers and grass are growing, and then look at those wild chokecherry trees and wild yellow-currant bushes on the hills. I am sure that the dirt is rich enough for a fine garden."

Pa looked at her all the time that she talked. He frowned and pinched his lips together. Then he smiled. Again he shook hands with the two miners.

CHAPTER 3

Red-Flannel Mine

Pa and Daniel took care of the animals while Ma and Betsy began to plan the meal. Then Pa walked over to the edge of the creek. He waited there while Daniel ran down to borrow Mr. Allred's extra gold pan. Daniel ran as fast as he could go. He was in a hurry to find some gold.

But he was not in too much of a hurry to watch Allred and Macgruder each pan a pan of sand. It was fun to see them put some dirt and gravel and water into the flat, dark-colored pan and pour off the water a little at a time.

"See how we do it?" asked Mr. Allred, shaking the pan back and forth. "We'll have a show of gold here in a little while. Think you could pan a pan of sand?"

Daniel nodded. He thanked them before he hurried off to meet Pa.

"Hm-m-m!" said Pa as they stood in the shade of the big pine tree and looked at the rushing water. "This creek is very swift. You and Betsy must be careful not to fall in. If you did, you would be carried far downstream."

Pa started to walk along the edge of the creek. Then he began to walk fast. He went faster and faster. Daniel's short legs had to hurry to try to keep up with Pa's long legs. Daniel began to puff. He felt very warm.

"Please, Pa," he begged. "Please don't walk so fast. I'm so hot and tired. And, oh, but how I wish that Ma would let me take off this heavy red flannel underwear. It makes me itch all over. I don't see why I have to wear it in the summertime. Red flannel underwear doesn't do anyone any good that I can see. I hate it!"

Daniel frowned as he bent over to scratch his legs. Pa smiled as he looked down at the little boy.

"We'll talk to Ma tonight about making a change to lighter underclothes, Danny," he answered. "Ma does not want you to take cold in this higher climate. And it is chilly here at night, even though it is June. But I think that the days are hot enough so that now we can safely pack away our winter clothes until fall. You will be glad to wear them then."

By this time they had reached a big, mossy log. Long ago it had fallen across the singing stream. It made a wide bridge. On the log, they could easily cross to the other side.

"I believe I'll use our gold pan right here first," said Pa, looking down at the creek bank just below them.

"Oh, Pa, why don't you cross over on the log and try the other side," Daniel cried. "I think that it looks much better over there. I know it does." He again eyed the opposite bank.

Pa chuckled. "Well, if you aren't a real gold miner already, I'll eat my old black hat," he replied.

But he shook his head.

"No, I think we'll begin our panning right here. Later on, we can work on the other side of the creek."

Pa started to go down the steep bank. Just as Daniel followed in his footsteps, Pa turned around. He hurried back up to the higher ground.

"Do you know, Son, I think I'd better go back and see how Ma and Betsy are getting along with the wood for the campfire. I'm afraid that your Ma will work too hard. And we don't want her to get sick again just when she is really getting well and strong. I'll walk back to the wagon and see if any help is needed. Then I'll come back here. Do you want to go with me, or do you want to wait?"

"I'll wait here, Pa, if you don't mind. Maybe I can cool off a little by the time you get back."

"All right, Danny. But mind, now, don't you get too near that water," said Pa.

After Pa left, Daniel again looked across the rushing water. He looked down at the gold pan that Pa had left on the grass. Then he stared at the big, mossy log far above the singing stream.

Pa had said that he must not get too near the water. But if he crossed on the big log bridge, he would not be so very near to the hurrying mountain stream.

He had a plan in mind. Oh, he could not wait to try out his plan. How pleased Pa would be if he could have this nice surprise ready for him when he came back from the wagon.

Yes, he would do it! He would leave the heavy gold pan on this creek bank, but he would cross over on the log to the other side. There he would scoop up some of the dirt. Carefully, he would bring back this dirt and dump it into the flat pan. Then perhaps by the time Pa returned, he would have the surprise all ready to show him.

Quick as a flash, Daniel crawled out on the log. It was big and firm. It did not move one inch. Halfway across he stopped a minute to look down into the fast-moving water far below. He felt dizzy. He lay flat down on the log and shut his eyes tight.

"You're a baby," he told himself. "And you can't be a gold miner if you act like a baby."

He opened his eyes, but he did not look down into the water. He pulled himself up on his knees and stared straight ahead as he crawled the rest of the way across the log.

How good the hard ground felt. He dug his heels into the dirt as he jumped up and down two or three times. Then he leaned over and pushed one hand deep into the earth. Yes, it was exactly like the dirt that Mr. Allred had panned. He would take some back with him.

He reached into his pocket with his clean hand. He tried to pull out his handkerchief. No handkerchief was there. He reached down deeper. But there was nothing in his pocket except a colored rock and a piece of dried-up moss.

He had forgotten to bring anything in which to carry back the dirt and gravel. And if he did not hurry, Pa would come back. And then his surprise would be spoiled.

Suddenly he nodded his head. Why wouldn't that do? Quickly he slipped out of his pants. He spread them out on the ground. Next, he scooped up the dirt from the edge of the creek. He piled it into his pants. They made a very good sack.

He gathered up his load of dirt and ran back to the log bridge. The surprised birds in the cottonwood and pine trees flew from branch to branch when they saw the little boy in his bright red flannel underwear.

"Tweet, tweet. Chee-chee. Tweet, tweet," they called to each other as they fluttered their wings.

This time Daniel ran bravely across the log. He dumped out some of the dirt and gravel into the gold pan. He ran down to the creek and put in some water. Then he knelt down and began to shake the pan back and forth and from side to side. Sloosh. Spill. Sloosh. Spill. The water whirled round and round in the flat pan, and every now and then some of it spilled out over the pan's edge.

The sun was hot upon Daniel's back. The red

flannel underwear was even hotter. But he worked with such great interest that he soon forgot everything but panning for gold.

He jumped to his feet at Pa's loud shout. He almost dropped the pan. Pa's strong hands grabbed the pan and saved the gold from spilling.

"Well, I do declare," Pa said slowly. "So this is what you've been doing while I've been gone." Pa's wise, kind eyes looked from Daniel's wet, muddy trousers to the log and back again to the shine of gold in the bottom of the dark pan.

"Well, I do declare," Pa said again. "I wonder how much gold is in here." He did not say one word about Daniel going across the log or using his good clothes for a sack. But Daniel began to wonder what Ma would say to him. Perhaps his idea had not been such a good one, after all.

"Let's take your panning down and ask our new friends about it, Son," he finally said.

Daniel was off with a jump. He was a scarlet streak in the sunshine as he ran through the tall grass.

He was stopped short by the men's roar of laughter. He looked down at himself. And then he remembered. Here he was, running about in broad daylight with only his flannel underwear for a covering.

"Why, Daniel Lane!" exclaimed Ma. She hurried over to him. "What in the world have you been doing?"

"Daniel Lane!" shouted Betsy. She looked at him with wide-open eyes. "You ought to be ashamed of yourself. That's what you ought to be."

"Oh, let the boy alone," said Mr. Allred, wiping his eyes. He had laughed until he cried. He chuckled as he again looked at the red flannel underwear. "He ought to be my boy," he said. "It looks as though he is ALL-RED, too."

Then Mr. Allred looked carefully into the gold pan which Pa handed to him. He gently shook it back and forth.

"Hmm-m-m," he said. "You'll feel pretty happy when I tell you how much gold Danny has panned out here."

"Does it really amount to very much?" asked Pa anxiously. He leaned closer to again look into the pan.

"That's a mighty good show for a little work, if you ask me," spoke Macgruder.

"Yes, sir, it is," added Allred. "This show of gold right here is worth at least two dollars. Maybe it'll be worth more than that when it is weighed out on the scales."

"Two dollars!" exclaimed Ma. "Perhaps we will get enough gold so that someday, when I am well and strong, we can buy another farm in the Willamette Valley."

"Yes, ma'am," agreed Macgruder. "I think that maybe you can. For it looks as though Daniel has struck some rich pay dirt. I think the boy has found a good claim, Lane. You'd better get it staked out right now."

"And choose a name for your claim, too," said Allred. "You should have a name when you file your claim at the county seat. Can you think of a good name?"

Pa began to laugh. He laughed and laughed for a long time before he could say one word.

"Yes, I've got a name for the Lane's gold mine," Pa finally said. He pointed to Daniel. "We'll name it for our boy. And we'll get rid of his heavy winter underwear and hang it there for a marker."

"That's just what we'll do," said Ma. They both smiled at Daniel.

"You found our claim, Son, and I'm going to name it for you," said Pa. "From now on we'll call it the RED FLANNEL MINE."

CHAPTER 4

Muslin Town

After the excitement of finding their claim, it was some time before the Lane family could settle down to eat the good dinner that Ma and Betsy had cooked.

"This is the first time that I was ever so slow in coming to eat your sourdough biscuits, Ma," said Pa. "You have cooked a fine meal for us."

"You must thank Betsy, too," said Ma, smiling. "While you and Daniel were staking the Red Flannel Mine, we were busy planning our new home. We are anxious to put up our tent and set our stove in one corner so that I can really do some baking again. Some dried-peach pies would taste good for a change."

Pa looked at Ma in surprise. "Tent?" he questioned. "Where will we get a tent? We are many, many miles from any store."

Ma and Betsy looked at each other and smiled.

"Why, Joseph," answered Ma, "don't you remember all that muslin that I bought in Eugene City just before we left? I brought it along to use in my sewing. It is such strong, long-wearing cloth that I bought several bolts of it. We will use that muslin for our tent."

"Well, I do declare," said Pa. "I can see that you and Betsy have been very busy making plans."

"Yes, we have," Ma laughed. "And you and Danny will be busy, too. For there are plenty of small trees all around us that can be cut down and used for poles to make a tent framework. We will stretch the muslin cloth over the tent poles. Then we can unload our furniture and once more live in a house. Only this will not be a wooden house. It will be a muslin house."

Betsy clapped her hands. "That is what we will name this place, Ma," she cried.

"Why, child, what do you mean?" asked Ma.

"That's what we'll name this camping place. Mr. Allred and Mr. Macgruder told us that soon many people will come here. They will come just as soon as they hear about the gold that all of us have found. And because there are no houses here, those people will have to live in tents, too."

Betsy again clapped her hands. "Don't you see, Ma? This is Muslin Town. We'll all be living in Muslin Town."

Ma's eyes sparkled. She turned to Pa and nodded her head.

"Betsy is right, Pa," she agreed. "That is a very fine name. Danny gave our mine a fine name, too."

"Yes," said Pa, "it is a good name. MUSLIN TOWN and RED FLANNEL MINE are both good names."

Ma and Betsy hurried to finish the dishes so that all of them could choose a place to put up their tent. They looked here, and they looked there. They saw many beautiful spots. But at last Pa and Ma and Daniel and Betsy chose a shady place on the sloping hillside. And here Pa began to build the framework for the tent house.

At last the white muslin house was finished. It looked fresh and clean. Then they began to unpack the furniture from the covered wagon. There were three special pieces that were unpacked first of all.

The first piece to be taken inside was a small cook-stove that they had used in the farm home in the Willamette Valley.

"I could cook over a campfire all the time if I had to," Ma told Pa. "But I am glad that I don't have to." So they had brought the little stove.

The second piece to be carefully carried inside was the little rosewood melodeon that had first come all the way west across the plains with Ma. Now it had come back east of the mountains with her.

She untied the big quilt which was wrapped around it. Right then and there she sat down on the little stool. She opened the hinged lid and put her fingers on the ivory keys. She put her feet on the small pedals and began to pump them up and down, up and down.

Soft, sweet music came out of the little organ. Daniel and Betsy and Pa stood back of Ma until she finished playing. They all loved the music of the little melodeon. It always sent happy chills up and down the children's backs.

"That is enough playing for now," said Ma, gently closing the shining, hinged lid. "But tonight I will play some hymns for our evening worship, and we will sing them."

The third piece of furniture to be carried carefully into the tent was the bird's-eye maple chest of drawers that Grandpa had built before Ma was born. Grandpa and Grandma had given the bird's-eye maple chest and the rosewood melodeon to Ma, for her wedding presents when she and Pa were married back East.

Ma had often told Daniel and Betsy how she and Pa had walked many miles across the plains when they came west, rather than have to take the beautiful chest and the melodeon out of the heavily loaded wagon and leave them beside the trail.

How glad Daniel and Betsy were that Pa and Ma had been able to bring these things all the way to Oregon. Now they had them here in Muslin Town.

After the stove and the melodeon and the maple chest were in the tent, they brought in the mattresses and the bedding. They brought in the dishes and the books and the pictures and all the things that a family needed to make a real home.

"I don't think that anyone who comes here will have a nicer home than we do," Betsy said proudly that night as she snuggled down in the mattress of fresh-smelling wild hay.

"It'll be just fine when I have time to make some furniture, Little Chick," said Pa. "We'll have a big table and benches and bedsteads, too. Yes, sir, we'll even have bookshelves for our books. It's a good thing that I brought along all my carpenter's tools."

Daniel and Betsy were almost too busy to play at all during the next few days.

Each morning Betsy helped Ma get breakfast and do the dishes. She fed and watered the proud, crowing rooster and the fat, cackling hens while Pa and Daniel tended to the livestock.

Then Pa and Daniel panned a few pans of sand each morning and early afternoon. Sometimes they worked and worked without even getting a show of color. But other times they had very good luck. The little sacks of gold dust were getting fuller and heavier. Pa said that at last it looked as though the Lanes were really going to be rich, for he was sure that their claim was one of the best on the creek.

"And now that my biggest lump of gold is getting well and strong, I can be very happy," Pa said. He always looked at Ma when he talked about his biggest lump of gold. Her cheeks always turned pink, and her eyes sparkled as she said, "Oh, Joseph Lane, how you do talk!"

Late afternoon was the time Pa and Daniel worked on the furniture for their tent house. When it was finished, Ma said that she had never had a finer table or benches or shelves.

And she knew that when Pa finished the little high-backed rocking chair with the curved arms and the rawhide seat, she would like it better than any chair she had ever seen. She would sit in it in the evening and look across the quiet valley.

But long before the little rocking chair was finished their green valley was no longer quiet. Pa and Ma and Daniel and Betsy could look out of their tent any day and see wagons winding around the mountainsides. Many men rode into the valley on horseback. Some men walked in, leading mules loaded with their food and clothing.

Pa said that he did not see how three hundred people could have found out so quickly about the gold. In only a few weeks time the banks of the pretty little creek were lined with tents.

"You were right, Betsy," said Pa. "This really has become Muslin Town."

Every day Daniel and Betsy walked up and down past the tents, hoping that they would find some new family with children. But always they were disappointed to find that there were no children. Only the men had come first, to see if they could find gold. It was over a year before the first families came in by wagon train from California. At that time fourteen women and a few children came with the men. What a happy day that was for Daniel and Betsy.

And so the time passed by. They were busy, happy days. And they were golden days, too, for almost every afternoon, Pa and Daniel added to the growing bags of gold dust which soon Pa would have to take out over the long, rough trail to The Dalles. There he would have the bags weighed, and he would be given money for his gold dust.

**They were disappointed to find
that there were no children.**

Daniel and Betsy loved to walk past the long rows of tents and look at the people who filled the town. There were Indians, and red-shirted miners, and soldiers who shouted above the noise of the braying mules and the stamping of horses' hooves.

It was not long until Pa said that they would have to stuff bags full of sand so that they would not be hit by stray bullets.

"Fill bags with sand, Pa?" Betsy asked in wonder. "But we can't carry those heavy sacks of sand around in front of us wherever we go! I'd surely drop mine."

"Pooh!" sniffed Daniel. "Isn't that just like a girl? Of course you wouldn't carry a sandbag around with you, silly. Pa means that we'll put the bags around our beds at night. Then, if any bullets come through the canvas part of our walls, they'll land in the sandbags instead of in us. It won't hurt the sand any. But it wouldn't do us much good to have a few bullet holes in us."

"Do you really think we need to do that, Joseph?" asked Ma, her eyes wide and frightened.

"Yes, it would be a good idea," Pa answered. "It can't do any harm, and it might do a lot of good. A sleeping soldier got hit in the arm by a flying bullet just last night. That's what gave me the idea of sleeping behind these bags."

Betsy looked sober that night when she crawled over the sandbags to get into her bed. She reached out and touched them. Some of the sandbags had little sacks of gold dust hidden in their fat middles.

"As long as we have to use them for safety, we might as well use them as banks, too," Pa told them. "We're getting so much gold dust that we'll have to hide it somewhere."

Betsy giggled as she looked down at Calico Cat and Rags curled up on the cowhide rug beside the beds.

"What's the matter?" sleepily asked Daniel from his bed right next to hers.

"Oh, nothing," she replied. "Except that I was thinking of all the funny things we'll have to tell Grandpa and Grandma when we see them. Danny, just think of sleeping with bags and bags of gold dust piled all around near us."

Danny opened his mouth to answer, but his words were drowned in the deafening clatter of horses' hooves on the stony path outside. Wild yells split the quiet night.

"Yipee! Ki-Yi!" yelled a dozen rough voices as rowdy horsemen dashed past the Lane's tent.

"Yipee! Ki-Yi!" again they shouted. Pistol shots cracked.

Ping!

Betsy screamed, Rags barked, and both landed in a heap on Pa and Ma's bed.

Ping! Plunk!

"What's the matter? What is it, Pa?" cried Danny, springing out and grabbing Pa's hand.

"Under the beds, all of you," quickly ordered Pa.

In the darkness Daniel and Betsy clung tightly to Rags and Calico Cat. They trembled until Ma's soft voice quieted their fast-beating hearts.

"Don't be afraid, children. We are safe here. Those were only a few careless miners out for a good time. They did not mean to shoot anyone."

"Just the same, it's lucky for us that we had these sandbags here," added Pa soberly. "The 'ping' that you heard was a stray bullet whizzing into our tent house, and the 'plunk' was the thud of that same bullet as it buried itself in this sandbag right over Betsy's head."

They did not crawl out of their shelter until the night was quiet once again.

"Well," sighed Betsy, "now I guess we'll *really* have something to tell Grandpa and Grandma. But this wasn't so funny, was it?"

Danny chuckled a sleepy chuckle. "No, it wasn't funny, Betsy. But it certainly was exciting. I guess this proves that almost anything can happen in Muslin Town!"

CHAPTER 5

Winter

"Oh, Danny, come and look! Look at that big flock of geese flying over." Betsy pointed at a dark wedge in the blue sky.

"Yes, and they are headed south. That means that winter will soon be here. Pa said only yesterday that the ducks and geese would soon be going south to spend the winter."

"I hope Pa will go south, too," Betsy added. "Ma said most of the miners were going to California to stay until spring. They made a rule that no one can jump their claims while they are gone. If we go to California, maybe you and I could go to school. It would be more fun than saying our lessons to Ma. Let's beg Pa to go to California, Danny."

"It won't do any good. I heard Pa tell Mr. Allred that he could save more money by staying here this winter. Besides, Ma said she wasn't strong enough to travel so far."

Betsy looked out across the brown hills. Far to the south was California. Her mother had told her that it was a beautiful land with trees and fruit and flowers. To the west, across the high mountains, was the Willamette Valley. There were Betsy's friends and playmates. There were towns and villages with schools and stores and churches. Here, before her, lay only miles of land and the dirty muslin tents of the miners' camp.

"Oh, if I could only be a goose!" Betsy said softly. "I'd fly away and take all of the family with me."

"Goosey, goosey, goo-sey!" Daniel cried, and he began to dance around his sister and crook his finger in her face. "You are a goose if you want to leave here. I want to stay so we can get a lot of gold and then buy us a big farm."

That night Betsy lay awake in her little bed on the frame of cottonwood poles. She heard her mother and father talking.

"We can get enough whip-sawed lumber for a small house," said her father.

Betsy knew about whip-sawed lumber. She had watched two men sawing boards one day. It took them a long time to saw a thin plank off of the log. The log lay upon two heavy sawhorses. One man stood on top of the log. The other one stood under the log. They pulled the long saw back and forth, back and forth. It looked like hard work!

"We can't pay three hundred dollars for a thousand feet of that whip-sawed lumber," her mother answered. "At that price, a small cabin would cost us a thousand dollars. We just can't spend our money that way."

"We must have a better shelter than this muslin tent. Winters are cold here—much colder than over in the country west of the Cascades."

"I have an idea!" Mrs. Lane said at last. "Why not use that cave that you and the children dug in the side of the hill when you were following that vein of gold? You could make it a little larger and set up the tent in front. I think we could make a very cozy place if we tried."

The very next day, the Lane family set to work on the cave. When it was big enough, Pa cut pine poles and made a wall across the front with a door which he made from some whip-sawed lumber. The door fastened with a latch which slipped back and forth. Ma and Betsy twisted the cord through a hole in the door.

"Now our latch string hangs on the outside," Pa said. "All who want to enter may pull the string, lift the latch, and come in."

"Suppose some bad white man or unfriendly Indians should come!" Betsy exclaimed.

"Then we could lock the door by pulling the latch string inside," Daniel explained. "No one can open the door from the outside unless the latch string hangs out. See!" Danny proudly showed his sister how the latch worked.

Grandpa Green from the Apple Cider Mine helped to build the fireplace and the chimney. Rocks which had been thrown aside from the gold miners were used, and the job was soon finished.

When the work was all done, the Lanes began to move right into their new home in the cave. It was a good thing, too, because that very night a cold wind began to howl, and, as Danny said, "Winter came in a hurry."

Outside the wind blew and made ugly, lonesome noises as it whistled through the canyon. Inside the cave, the Lane family was cozy and warm.

The fire burned cheerily, and after a good supper of hot mush and fresh milk, the family sat around the fire and talked. Ma told the children all she knew about the cave dwellers who lived long, long ago.

"I'm glad we have a cave and are going to stay right here in it this winter," Betsy said. "We are just like the cave dwellers. Of course, our cave is much nicer. We have Ma's maple chest and her melodeon, and our cook-stove. I'm sure the cave dwellers didn't have nice things like these."

"It's growing late, children," Ma said. "Let's have our family prayers and go to bed. Betsy, you may hold the candle so that I can see how to play the melodeon."

Ma chose a hymn about "safe from the storms that toss the waves." Pa read a chapter from the Bible that told how to build a house on a good foundation so that the wind would not blow it away. When Betsy said her prayer, she added a new line: "Thank Thee, Father, for our warm cave and its strong door."

Days flew by. Pa and Daniel worked at panning gold when the weather was warm enough. One day when it was too cold to work outside, Pa dug a big hole in the back of their cave. "That's the pantry," he explained. "Nothing can freeze in there."

Ma and Betsy cooked and washed and kept the cave home neat and clean. When all the work was done, they knitted. It took warm socks and stockings and mittens and caps for such cold weather. There were no stores where such things could be bought.

One day a strange man rode into Muslin Town. Pa and Daniel were panning at the little stream. They looked up when they heard the sound of hooves on the rocky trail.

"There's a pack train coming to camp," the man shouted as he rode by. "It's just over the hill."

"What's a pack train, Pa?" Danny asked.

"You'll see, sonny! Bring the pan and come on. We will go and tell Ma and Betsy."

Soon the Lanes were standing on the hill above the cave, looking toward the north. All the other people of the camp were outside, too. After a while, Danny saw a tiny dark speck on a hill far away. Then he saw other specks—a long line of them.

"Here they come," Pa called, and waved his old black hat. The dark specks were horses and mules. As they came closer, Danny saw the canvas packs on their backs.

"Now I know what a pack train is," cried Danny. "The horses and mules are the train cars. What are they bringing in the packs, Pa?"

"Food and clothes and tools and the things which we need, sonny."

Daniel and Betsy Lane would never forget that day. They watched the men untie the big packs from the animals' backs and put them on the ground near one of the tents.

"Mail, mail, mail," yelled a man as he opened a pack and waved a bundle of letters above his head.

The people crowded around him. Daniel heard him call out the names and saw the hands of the miners reach up for their letters.

It had been many months since she had heard from her parents in the East. If he could only take a letter to Ma, how happy she would be!

**As they came closer, Danny saw
the canvas packs on their backs.**

Daniel watched the stack of mail grow smaller and smaller. At last there were only four messages left.

"Won Sing Lung. Jed Perkins. Tracy Merryweather, Esquire," he called out.

A slender little Chinese man, a husky red-shirted miner, and a tall, well-dressed gentleman with a sparkling diamond ring pushed through the crowd to claim their messages.

Daniel's eyes filled with tears. He turned his face away as the man held out the last letter.

"Mrs. Mary Lou Lane," called the man.

"That's my mother!" Danny cried and reached up a hand. "I'll take it to her."

Away ran Danny to his mother. "A letter! And it's for you, Ma!"

"Oh, thank you, Danny," Ma said. She took the letter and opened it with trembling fingers. "Run and tell your Pa that at last I have heard from my family."

That night Ma read the letter aloud. It was from her mother and father back in Virginia. The letter told about the war that was being fought back there between the Northerners and the Southern States. It said that Ma's brothers were all soldiers and had gone away to fight in the war.

There was good news, too. It was about a railroad which was being built all the way to California. When it was finished, Grandma wrote, she and Grandpa were going to come out West on a visit. Grandma said she was too old to make such a long trip in a covered wagon.

The next day Pa brought a good many things from the men of the pack train. He bought a small shovel and a gold pan for Danny and a pair of boots with copper pieces over the toes.

For Betsy he bought a piece of beautiful wool cloth. Mother said it would be just enough for a skirt. He bought a shiny kettle for Ma and a big blue bowl. He bought sugar, bacon and coffee and salt and a big sack of dried beans.

Ma bought some things, too. Betsy saw her tucking them away in the top drawer of the maple chest. She wanted to know what her mother was hiding, but she did not find out for a long time.

When Christmas came, there was a little doll for Betsy, a tin top for Daniel, and a storybook for each of them. Then Betsy knew what Mother had hidden away in the chest.

CHAPTER 6

Garden On Gold Mountain

"I've heard of grass in the garden," said Pa one day in the spring. "But I never heard of a garden in the grass."

"Well, just you wait," replied Ma. "We will show you one. If bunchgrass can grow here so well, other things can, too. My children must have some fresh vegetables. Just see how pale they look."

"But where will you get garden seed?" Pa asked.

"I have them tucked away. I brought them along just in case we should find a place where we could grow a garden." Ma patted Pa's hand. "If you'll just stop digging and panning long enough to help us clear a garden place, we won't ask you to help any more."

That very afternoon Ma came down to the creek where Pa and the children were washing sand for gold. Ma sat on a stump and watched.

"See, Ma," Daniel said as he wiped his dirty hand across his sweat-streaked face. "This rocker Pa made is lots faster than just using the gold pan. Betsy and I put the sand in the rocker. We shoved it into this box of a thing. Betsy dips up some water and pours it into the box, and then Pa begins to rock it back and forth. You see, it slopes toward the creek so that the water runs out at that end. As Pa rocks the rocker back and forth, the sand is washed out with the water. The gold settles to the bottom because it is heavier than the sand and gravel."

"Then comes the most exciting part," Betsy put in. "Then Pa cleans out all of the sand and gravel that has settled against the little slats on the bottom of the rocker. He puts it in a gold pan and washes it again. Danny and I watch for a show of colors. Sometimes there isn't any, sometimes just a little bit, but sometimes there is good, coarse gold."

"Like this, Ma." Danny picked up a tin can from beside a log. He held it up for Ma to see. The can was half full of golden grains. Ma turned the can and watched them sparkle in the sun.

"Gold is a fine thing," Ma said. "But only because of the fine things it can buy—only because of the good that it can do for people. Some people come to the gold fields and find great fortunes. Some of them spend their riches foolishly and get only bad things for their gold. We have seen that happen right here in Muslin Town. Don't work too hard, Joseph. We want only enough gold to buy us a home again—only enough to buy us the things that we should have. Our health and our happiness are worth more than all the gold in eastern Oregon."

Pa laid down the shovel. He took out his old red handkerchief and mopped his face.

"Where do you want that garden, Mary Lou?" Pa asked simply.

Ma selected a place just below the flume that took water from the creek to a dry gulch where some men from California had staked their claims.

"Too bad that we can't hope to use some of that precious water when the days get hot and our garden gets dry," Ma said sadly.

All the next day, Pa and the children worked hard at clearing the sloping hillside. Luckily, no one had thought it a likely spot for gold, so very few holes had been dug there. Of course, these had to be leveled, the small trees had to be taken out, the bushes grubbed up, and the bunchgrass dug up and burned.

The following day Betsy was helping cook dinner. She saw Ma take a small bag out of the pantry.

"Oh, potatoes," cried Betsy. "Good, good potatoes. Can we cook a lot of them, Ma? I'm so hungry for some."

"Only a few, dear. We must make them last."

Betsy watched Ma as she took a sharp knife and cut little chunks out of the potatoes. These she carefully put into a basket.

"We'll cut the eyes out of the potatoes," she explained. "We will plant the eyes to make more potatoes. We will eat only the center part."

"Oh, Ma, that's a funny way to do it. Pa used to plant whole potatoes when we lived in the Willamette Valley."

"Yes, but they are very scarce here in Muslin Town. We must be very saving with the few that I bought from the pack train. These are very expensive potatoes. They have kept very well in the pantry your Pa made. We will have many eyes to plant and some pieces to eat."

The potatoes were carefully planted in the soft, moist garden soil, and before Betsy knew it, little green leaves were pushing up through the ground.

One day Betsy and Ma picked a basket of green beans from the vines in the garden.

"I'm afraid this is all the beans we will ever get, Betsy," Ma said sadly. "It's like your Pa said, you can't make a garden grow in this country without water."

Betsy made marks in the dusty soil with her bare toes and wished and wished it would rain.

At noon Danny ate so many green beans that Ma said that he would be sick. She was right. In the middle of the night, she had to get up and give him some soda water.

The next morning she said to Pa, "Joseph, I thought sure I smelled rain last night when I was up with Daniel."

Pa laughed. "I'm afraid you were dreaming, Mary Lou. The cow pen was dry as a bone when I went out to milk Mercy-Me this morning. Even the water trough was dry. Run to the creek, Daniel, and get a bucket of cool water for the thirsty cow. Your breakfast can wait. After all of those beans you ate yesterday, you should not be very hungry this morning."

Pa had just finished saying the blessing when Danny ran up to the door as fast as his bare feet could carry him.

"Ma, you're right!" he shouted. "It did rain last night. The garden is all muddy. See!"

Danny's feet were covered with mud.

"Oh, yes, I see," said Pa. "I see what has happened. There is a break in that flume above us, and the water has run out all over your garden. It will have to be fixed as soon as we eat. The miners below can't work without water."

Ma was sorry for the miners, but she was glad her precious garden was wet. Now it would not die. Her children would have good vegetables, and maybe there would be some to spare.

While Pa repaired the flume, Daniel rode Old Hope down to tell the miners what had happened. He liked to do things like that. It made him feel like he was really growing up.

One night in the late fall, Daniel was awakened by the sound of hooves striking against the rocks on the mountainside. He tried to go back to sleep. He turned his face toward the smooth dirt wall of the cave and covered his ear with his pillow. Then he sat up quickly.

He must find out what it was! Wasn't he the man of the house now?

Quickly he crawled out of bed and slipped into his pants.

Pa had ridden Hope to The Dalles with a pack train and had told Danny that he would have to look after Ma and Betsy and take care of things while he was gone. All of the miners who lived near the cave had gone over to another camp to some kind of a meeting.

Danny felt very important. He hurried out as quietly as he could so as not to awaken his mother.

It was a dark night. At first Danny could see only the black shape of things. There was the big stack of wild hay that he and Pa had cut and stacked during the summer. It was for the cow and the horse and the old oxen to feed on if snow came and covered the grass so that they could not graze. This had happened to many animals last year, in the terrible winter of 1861-1862.

Danny went to the little pole pen where Mercy-Me was kept at night. Perhaps she had pushed the poles over and was running around on the hillside. Perhaps it was her hooves that he had heard.

Yes, the cow was gone!

He hurried back to the cave. Betsy would have to help find Mercy-Me.

Soon the two children were on their way to look for her. If she strayed away too far, an Indian would be sure to steal her. Then there would be no more good milk and butter for the Lane family.

It was a warm night. Betsy slipped out in her long white muslin nightgown, with only her little shawl around her shoulders.

"Let's stand still and listen," whispered Betsy. "Maybe we can hear her walking and tell which way she is going."

The lonesome howl of a coyote far away on a hilltop was the only sound they heard.

In a moment Danny cried, "There she is, over that way! I hear her!"

"That's more than one cow," Betsy said. "Sounds like a bunch of cattle or horses to me."

"Maybe it's the men coming back."

"Or Indians!" gasped Betsy as she grabbed Danny's arm.

"It is! That's just what it is. Indians are driving off the horses and cattle!"

For a moment the children clung to each other in the darkness.

"Look out, Danny! Here they come, right this way."

"Oh, Betsy, they are going to run right through Ma's garden. That little picket fence won't keep them out."

Indians are driving off the horses and cattle.

"Head them off!" shouted Betsy. "Head them off! They will step on everything!"

She began to yell and scream and wave her shawl above her head. Danny jumped up and down and clapped his hands against his legs. Rags ran bravely back and forth and barked with all his might.

The horses didn't like the jumping, yelling children and the angry, yipping dog. They turned before they reached the garden and went snorting and clattering on around the hill.

Just as Ma hurried out into the night to see what was wrong, two men on horseback turned their horses and dashed away into the darkness.

"We saved the garden, Ma," Betsy cried.

"Here's old Mercy-Me coming back to her pen," Daniel shouted. "With Tick and Tack tagging right along behind her."

"You brave children! You scared those pesky Indian thieves away and kept them from stealing all those cows and horses," Ma said proudly as she put her arms around Daniel and Betsy.

CHAPTER 7

A New Betsy Ross

"Muslin Town is going to have a big celebration on Thanksgiving Day," said Pa one night at the supper table. "There will be a big parade, and music, and they say they have invited the Governor of Oregon to come over and make a speech."

"Oh, that will be fine," said Ma. "Muslin Town has grown so fast. I think they could have a real good celebration."

"Will they ask the Indians to come like the Pilgrims did at the first Thanksgiving?" Betsy asked.

"Oh, yes, the friendly ones are all invited. Chief Little Eagle is going to bring his whole tribe and camp down in the valley."

Daniel and Betsy worked hard the next few weeks. Plans for the Thanksgiving celebration danced through their heads as they worked. Ma said the winter vegetables must be stored. They pulled carrots, parsnips, and turnips and stored them in the pantry. Ma picked seeds and carefully tied them up in little bags. These would plant next year's garden.

Pa quit working at his Red Flannel Mine long enough to dig the potatoes. Danny and Betsy carried them up to the cave.

The pantry was full at last. Outside the cave there were two baskets of potatoes, one small basket of onions, and two piles of pumpkins.

"We have stored all that we can use," said Ma. "We can sell these things that are left over to other people. The day of the celebration will be a good time to sell them."

One day Betsy came in from play to find her mother looking at a piece of blue cloth.

"Oh, Ma," cried Betsy. "Are you going to make my blue skirt for Thanksgiving?"

"I had planned to," Ma answered. "But I am afraid I can't."

"What's the matter, Ma? Don't you feel well?"

"No, it isn't that. I am feeling fine. The blue cloth is ruined, dear. I guess a mouse got into that box and cut holes in it. Just look!"

Ma held up the blue cloth. It was a sorry sight.

Betsy wiped her eyes and tried hard to grin so that the tears would not come. She smoothed the soft blue cloth and then spoke.

"It's such a pretty blue, just the color of the blue in the flag we had at our school in the valley. It was the United States flag that our teacher brought across the plains in a covered wagon."

That night as she dried the dishes for her mother, Betsy asked a question.

"Ma, does Muslin Town have a flag—a flag of the United States, I mean?"

"I have never seen one here, Betsy."

"Don't you think we should have a flag for the celebration?"

"It would be nice. Oregon is a state of the United States now, you know. We really should have a flag. But it is too late to send for one now."

Betsy dried the last plate.

"Ma, could you make a flag with all the stripes in it and all the stars on a field of blue?"

"Oh, I suppose I could—if I had the right colors of cloth."

It was the very next afternoon that Betsy came running in with a bundle under her arm.

"Here's the cloth, Ma. Here's the cloth for our flag!" she called out happily.

She dumped the bundle on the bed. Out rolled two white shirts with stiff, starched fronts, a white linen tablecloth, and a bright red silk dress.

"Where did you get all these things, Betsy?" Ma gasped.

"The sheriff gave me the two white shirts. He said he wouldn't need them anymore. Grandpa Green gave me the tablecloth. It was Grandma Green's before she died. He said she brought it all the way from Ireland. When I told him that Muslin Town needed a flag now that Oregon was a part of the United States, he went right over to his old leather-covered trunk. He took out this tablecloth and said he knew Grandma would be mighty proud to have it used in a flag."

"But the red silk dress? Where did you get it?"

"Oh, I had an awful time finding any red that was just right for the flag. I asked nearly everyone I saw. Then I met the preacher, and he said he thought he knew where I could get something. He took me down to the Greasy Platter Cafe and

**Muslin Town needed a flag now that
Oregon was a part of the United States.**

talked to one of the girls who works there. She went right back to her room and got me this red silk dress."

"But what about the blue?"

Then Ma's eyes twinkled, and she patted Betsy's head. "Oh, I know," she said. "The blue cloth that would have been your new skirt. It's a shame that the mouse ruined that skirt." Ma took the blue cloth from the top drawer of her maple chest. "If I had only put it in here at first, the mouse would not have found it."

"But if the mouse had not made the holes, I would not have thought about the flag," Betsy replied cheerfully.

The great day came at last. The morning was crisp and cool, but the sun was shining as bright as could be. Not many miners went to their diggings that day. Muslin Town was a very busy place. People hurried here and there, calling out friendly greetings to each other. Ribbons of smoke rose from the campfires of the Indians in the valley below the town. Young Indian braves dashed around the hillsides, trying out their ponies for the races.

Early that morning Pa had helped the children set up a sort of a "store" outside the tent. They used Ma's wash bench for a counter on which to show off the vegetables. Ma gave them the blue bowl to put their money in. Betsy had on her best calico dress and her high-top black shoes. She had rubbed them with a meat skin to make them look shiny. Danny was all cleaned up, too. He had on his gray wool pants with three white buttons sewed near his knees. He wore the long brown stockings which Betsy had knitted for him. He had on his copper-toed boots.

"It's too bad that Ma doesn't feel like helping us," Betsy said to Danny. The first rush of business was over, and they were waiting for more buyers to come.

Danny nodded and began to count the money in the blue bowl.

"Fifteen, sixteen, seventeen," he said. "Seventeen dollars already," he whispered.

A tall man with black whiskers walked up to the "store."

"How much are your potatoes?" he asked.

"Four for a dollar, sir," Betsy replied politely.

"They tell me that these vegetables grew right here in your garden," the man remarked as he picked up the potatoes.

"Yes, sir," Danny spoke up.

"Then that means that this country is good for something besides gold," the man said as he looked out toward the valley. "This gold will not last always. Gold fields soon play out. But if vegetables as fine as these will grow here, then other things will grow here, too. I'm going to start up a farm."

Before the children knew it, all the vegetables had been sold. The little "store" which Pa had set up for them had to be closed because there was nothing more to sell. Betsy and Daniel carried the blue bowl with all its money in to Ma, and then hurried away to be on hand for the parade.

Betsy thought it must be the grandest parade in all the world. The sheriff rode his shiny black horse. Chief Little Eagle rode beside him on his frisky painted pony. Behind them came a long string of men on horseback. One man with a funny clown suit and a painted face rode on a little donkey. On a wagon which was decorated with pine branches and bright paper flowers were several ladies with bright-colored dresses. Behind the wagon came the Indians—some riding, some walking—but all of them dressed in their beautiful, beaded buckskin clothes.

Betsy and Daniel had a good place on the hill where they could see everything. The parade wound through the narrow streets of Muslin Town and came to a stop at last just below them. Right in the spot where the garden had been, Pa had set up a tall pole. When Betsy asked him what it was for, he had said, "May use it next summer to scare off blackbirds."

Now Betsy knew he had been joking. The sheriff stopped beside the pole and took something from a package.

It was Betsy's flag. He raised his hat high above his head. The band stopped playing, and everyone was very quiet.

"Ladies and gentlemen," he said. "I have a gift for you. It is a gift from a little girl by the name of Betsy Lane. She is a second Betsy Ross because she has given Muslin Town its first flag. Hurrah for Betsy Ross Lane!"

A big cheer went up from the crowd. First a cheer for Betsy and then a cheer for the United States. Betsy couldn't remember just how it happened, but the next thing she knew, she was sitting right up on the sheriff's shiny black horse.

The band began to play, and the beautiful flag— Betsy's flag—waved proudly from the top of the high pole.

When the music ended, a man got up to make a speech. But Betsy didn't stay to hear what he said.

She just had to run home to thank her mother again for making the flag and to tell her all about the parade.

When Betsy reached the cave, she was surprised to find that the latch string was not hanging outside. She banged on the door and then listened for the sound of Ma lifting the latch.

But Betsy heard a new sound—a strange new sound. "Wah, wah, wah" it went.

What could it be?

Betsy beat on the door again, and then called out, "Ma, it's Betsy. Let me in."

The heavy door opened slowly. There stood Mrs. Brown from across the creek. In her arms she held a bundle wrapped in a white blanket.

"Land sakes, Betsy! Just guess what we've got here. Let me put it down so's you can get a good look." Mrs. Brown laid the bundle right over into Pa's old rocker that he had used all summer for washing out gold.

"This contraption makes a pretty fine cradle," said Mrs. Brown as she rocked it gently back and forth.

"Oh, it's a baby! A tiny little baby," Betsy cried. Then she looked at Ma.

"Yes, dear, it's a little baby sister for you and Daniel. Pa said it was surely a fine lump of gold we'd found this day."

Pa stood beside the bed and held Ma's white hand in his brown one. Ma smiled sweetly up at Betsy.

"We are going to let you name her, dear," she said.

"I've got a name all ready, Ma—a good name, too. Let's call her Goldie Lane."

"Get the Bible, Joseph, and write it down," Ma said.

"Wait, Pa, please wait. I want to run and find Danny first and let him give her a name, too. Our little sister must have two names."

When Daniel and Betsy came running into the cave, Danny took one look at his new baby sister and said, "Oh, Ma. I'm going to name her Thankful. Thankful Goldie Lane!"

Pa and Ma looked at each other and nodded.

"Well, bless me!" said Mrs. Brown as she smiled at the children. "That name suits just fine. Here's a golden-haired baby girl born in a mining camp. Rocked in a miner's pay dirt rocker. Born on Thanksgiving Day. In all the world you couldn't find a better name for the first baby born in Muslin Town."

The End